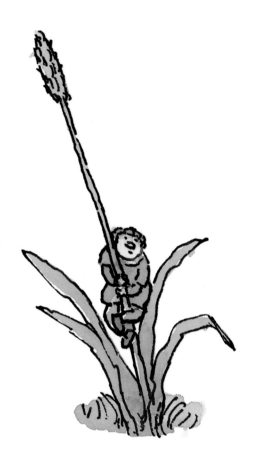

THE TOY BROTHER

William Steig

Michael di Capua Books

❧ ❧

HarperCollins Publishers

For Alicia, Ava Leigh, Courtney,
Emma, Graham, Kate, Kevin, Lily, Mariel,
Maya, Meaghan Rose, Peter, Timothy, Tomer, and Uri

Library of Congress catalog card number: 95-69464

Printed in the United States of America

Designed by Steve Scott

First edition, 1996

MAGNUS BEDE, the famous alchemist, and his happy-
go-lucky wife, Eutilda, thought they had a harmonious
family. But their older son, Yorick, considered little Charles
a first-rate pain in the pants, always occupied with something silly.

Mr. Bede made the mistake of allowing Yorick to be his apprentice. And Yorick got the notion that he would eventually surpass his father as an alchemist. He had visions of accomplishing such unheard-of miracles as turning plain old donkey dung into solid gold.

As for Charles, he spent his time chasing chickens, poking around in anthills, and arguing with the goat. He couldn't fathom why Yorick avoided him except to give him a wallop every now and then.

One May morning, Magnus and Eutilda were making ready to journey to a faraway wedding. Mrs. Bede reminded the boys to milk the goat and feed the animals. And Mr. Bede again warned Yorick: "Don't forget, you're still no alchemist. *So stay out of my lab!*"

The Bedes soon disappeared over the hill. They would not be back for at least a week.

Charles was glad Papa had forbidden Yorick the lab. He hoped that now, at last, they would get to be palsy-walsy, perhaps even do some chicken chasing together. But Yorick had other ideas.

So Charles went off on a ladybug hunt. He'd caught a couple when he spied something thrashing toward him through the weeds. He assumed it was a mole until he heard it saying, "It's me. Yorick. Your brother."

It was indeed Yorick, down to the minuscule wart on his knuckle!

"Egad," Charles gasped. "What happened to you?"

"What does it look like?" said Yorick.

"Don't tell me you snuck into father's laboratory!"

"Yes, goosewit," said Yorick, "and I invented a new potion. But when I tasted it, *za-zing!* I was no bigger than a cockroach. So I squoze under the door and here I am!"

Charles hastened inside to the kitchen, with Yorick clinging to his thumb squealing "Don't drop me, you dolt!"

It was just too marvelous. Yorick had made himself small as a sausage—and with only a drop of training.

"Stop staring, will you?" said Yorick. "I have to undo what I did or Papa will murder me. You've got to help."

"Okay, peanut, take it easy," said Charles. "There's still oodles of time till he gets home."

"Meanwhile," Charles announced, "I'm going to build you a house!"
"But what about the lab!"
"Don't rush me," said Charles. Humming happily, he set about making Yorick his very own house.

Charles was relishing this immensely. And when his toy brother stuck his head out the window of his new residence, it was all just as real as peas and beans.

"Brotherkins," Charles said, "it's dinnertime!" He served up three crumbs of bread and a spoonful of clabber cheese. He himself was too excited to eat a thing.

Running the show was so gratifying that Charles found himself wishing Yorick would fit in his pocket forever. Yes, it was rotten to be thinking this way, but how could he tell his brains how to operate?

In the morning, Charles decided Yorick needed some fresh air, so he took him out for a walk. Suddenly the sky darkened, the wind started howling, and they were pounded by hailstones as big as cherries. To Yorick they felt like cannonballs.

"Help!" he cried.

It finally struck Charles that his little bit of a brother would always be in danger. He could easily be stepped on by a donkey, even by his own dear mother. He could drown in a bucket of milk, get eaten by a thoughtless cat, or be seriously injured by a field mouse who was feeling his onions.

Charles didn't want any such thing to happen, even if it meant he'd have to be the baby again. He tucked his brother into his tunic and hurried home to put lard on his wounds.

"Yorick," he said, "we've got to make you big again. Let's get to work."

To make the time go faster, Charles tried to keep his brother amused. First, he dressed the goat up in one of his mother's best outfits, and then he squeezed the pig into his father's purple tunic.

But Yorick wasn't amused. He only wanted to be his real self again.

One night Yorick shook his brother awake and said, "What if I *never* get big again?"

"Yorks," said Charles, "I'm sure Pops can make you big again. But just in case he can't, and you have to stay in this condition, I'll take care of you as long as you live. Even after I get married, whether my wife likes it or not. And I mean it! So don't worry your little noggin."

At daybreak the boys heard familiar voices calling "Yo-o-or-keee! Cha-a-ar-leee!" They scrambled out of bed and out of the house, and there were their two parents! Charles got hugged and kissed again and again, as if they hadn't seen him for a year.

"And where's Yorick?" they wanted to know.

"Here he is!" Charles said, holding him up like a carrot.

The Bedes were bowled over. They stared. At tiny Yorick. At Charles. At the wide, mysterious heavens, and at each other. At last Mrs. Bede took up her son, kissed his little head, and held him to her bosom. "My chick," she sobbed, "my itty-bitty bantling."

"Alackaday," the father murmured, "what happened?" And Yorick, his flabbergasted parents hunched over him, told them his shameful story.

Magnus Bede carried his son straight to the laboratory. "Is your original potion still here?" he asked.

Yorick showed him the flask and everything he'd put in it: borage, betony, camphor, and sauerkraut.

"Don't worry," said Mr. Bede. "I can whip up the cure in a minute." But "the cure" had no effect.

"Are you sure you remembered everything, Yorick? Think!"

"Yes, Father, I did."

"Well, think harder! Something's got to be missing," said the famous alchemist. "The antidote isn't working."

Eutilda Bede cheerfully started making tiny clothes for her tiny son, a tiny bed with a tiny bedspread, a tiny chair with a cute little cushion. She cooked him tiny puddings and baked him dainty pies. Her new baby kept her too busy to worry.

"Tilda," Mr. Bede said finally, "I give up."

"Well," said his wife, "so he'll stay this way. Who cares? He's strong, handsome, and brave. *And* he has a fine horoscope."

"Let me drink some of Yorick's potion," Charles said. "Then we can be twins!"

"Gadzooks!" said Mrs. Bede. "What a noble idea! I'll drink it, too, and be a proper mother for you both. Perhaps Mr. Bede will join us, like a proper father."

"And WHO," Mr. Bede screamed, "will look after us minikins?"

Everyone clammed up.

That evening, after a supper consumed in silence, Mr. Bede said, "Son, I fear you are fated to be our little elf forever." And he sighed a long sorrowful sigh reeking of ginger.

"Ginger! Ginger!" Yorick cried. "I ate some ginger before I drank my awful potion!"

"Ah ha!" Magnus Bede exulted. "Ginger! That's a fish from another pond. Is it any wonder there was no transmogrification? *Now* I know what to do!"

They all ran to the lab.

There the truly wise alchemist took his original formula for restoring his son's stature and added pot cheese to counteract the ginger. He fed the mixture to Yorick, reciting these words: "Orknis-borknis, foofle-kedoofle, kefiffle-kefoffle-kefraffle-kafroom."

Magnus Bede chewing his lip, his wife chewing her nails, and Charles chewing her apron all stood goggle-eyed as Yorick swallowed the antidote, shivered, shook, and shot straight up to his full height.

Whereupon the whole Bede family, especially the proud father, went altogether out of their medieval minds. They hugged and kissed, wept, laughed, sang, yodeled, then raced around like a bunch of maniacs.

But Yorick still dreamed of turning donkey droppings into gold. And little Charles developed a passion for making toy dolls, which somehow all resembled Yorick.

The two brothers sincerely appreciated each other now.
Except when they were having a fight.